BILLY IS A BALLOON

CASSANDRA GAISFORD

DEDICATION

For my daughter Hannah—without whom this book would
never have been written
and for all the courageous children and adults
I have counselled
You inspire me

1

Billy is a balloon. When he goes to sleep, he releases all the old stagnant air.

When he wakes up, he lets all the old energy escape.

He goes outside and stretches wide.

He takes a great big gulp of fresh air and inhales it deep inside.

Deep, deep, deep into his lungs.
Deep, deep, deep into his heart.
Deep, deep, deep into his belly.
Deep, deep, deep into his feet.

Then whoosh! Whoosh! Whoosh!
        Billy draws the air up, up, up.
Up, up, up from his feet.
Up, up, up through his belly.
Up, up, up through his heart.
Up, up, up through his lungs.

4

But Billy didn't stop there.

He inhaled his big, beautiful breath up, up, up through his mouth, his lips, his nose.

Up, up, up through the middle of his eyes, his brows and his brain.

The air swirled through his body like a magic train.

Wow, look at me now! Look at me go!

5

Everything needs nurturing, especially me, he affirmed to himself, as he drew the air through the top of his skull and sent it sailing into the sky.

I am a balloon, he said, as he watched his beautiful, bright, breath fly by.

I can soar high, high, high up into the sky.

Or I can flop, low, low, low into the ground.

I can float, flip, and fly

Or I can drag, dip, and die

Die of boredom. Die of fatigue. Die of feelings I can never fly.

Billy bent down and touched his toes, then swung his body up and waved his hands into the sky.

I love life. I love living. I love. I love. I love. He cried. Love is the brightest energy ever to have lived.

I am a balloon and these are the things I love to do.

I love to write. I love to paint. I love to sew. I love to try things and do things I never thought I'd know.

I love to do the im-possible.

I'm possible to get up early out of bed.

I am possible to eat my breakfast of warm porridge and toasted bread.

I'm possible to fix my mind on places afar and dream and do the things that lift my horizons high and feeds my heart.

I FILL MY HEART, my hope, my happiness on all the places I want to go.

I float away from all the things that take me low.

Like fears and frights and feelings of failure.

Like meanies and critics and complainers.

Like too much distraction that sucks my energy.

I am a balloon. I need uplifting energy—not stagnant air.

8

———

"You are not a balloon. You're a stupid boy," Bella said one day.

Billy just smiled and floated away. Nope, he wasn't going to play with Bella today.

"You look silly," Sally said pointing at his yellow shirt and orange pants.

"I feel happy," Billy said as he floated away. Sally looked sad and mad, he thought looking down at her black shirt and black pants and the angry lines that darkened her face.

9

"Don't fly so high," Billy's mother scorned, as she tried to yank him down.

Billy smiled and waved and flew out of reach.

Out of reach from those who pulled him down.

Out of reach from those who only frowned.

Out of reach from his own mistaken beliefs.

Out of reach of all the toxic thoughts that limited his dreams.

"I CAN FLY. I can fly high, high, high. I have unlimited potential…

AND SO DO YOU! What colour is your balloon?

*** THE END ***

AUTHOR'S NOTE

Dear readers,

I wrote this book as I have so many of my books, for my daughter Hannah Joy. She messaged me on Anzac Day, during COVID-19, week six, feeling a little blue and saying she felt like it was Groundhog Day and it was hard to be motivated.

Motivated to finish the book she is writing.

Motivated to practice self-care.

Motivated to appreciate the gift sometimes hidden while the world is on pause.

One of the greatest gifts we can give our children and ourselves is the gift of self-reliance, fortitude, perseverance and courage.

Yes, we may be sociable people but we also have great power and resourcefulness to do things alone.

We can't wait for approval. We must give it to ourselves.

We can't wait for perfect timing. We must find it to ourselves.

We can't wait for inspiration. We must inspire ourselves.

We must, and we can, and we will, be a bright, beautiful, brilliant balloon.

We must fill our head, our heart, our lungs, our life, with all the things that feed our heart, nurture our minds, and nourish our souls. And we mustn't forget to breathe!

I created this book for my younger self. I made this book for you and your children. I wrote this book with love, and happiness, and glee.

Read this book at bedtime, at times of stress or pain or joy! I hope you find this book a great treasure trove of comfort. This book is always here for you—no matter what!

Stay in your bubble, dear readers. Soar High. Love who you are and who you can be.

Much love

P.S. **BILLY IS a Balloon** is now available in audio. Click here for your FREE copy>><u>https://dl.bookfunnel.com/znooq2ocme</u>

ABOUT THE AUTHOR

CASSANDRA GAISFORD is best known as *The Queen of Uplifting Inspiration.*

She is a holistic therapist, award-winning artist, and #1 bestselling author. A corporate escapee, she now lives and works from her idyllic lifestyle property overlooking the Bay of Islands in New Zealand.

Cassandra's unique blend of business experience and qualifications (BCA, Dip Psych.), creative skills, and wellness and holistic training (Dip Counselling, Reiki Master Teacher) blends pragmatism and commercial savvy with rare and unique insight and out-of-the-box-thinking for anyone wanting to achieve an extraordinary life.

ALSO BY THE AUTHOR

Stories and Fairytales

The Little Princess

I Have to Grow

The Little Boy Who Cried

The Little Princess Can Fly

Lulu Lost Her Confidence

Non-fiction Self-Empowerment Books

Mid-Life Career Rescue

How to Find Your Passion and Purpose

Bounce: Overcoming Adversity, Building Resilience and Finding Joy

Anxiety Rescue: How to Overcome Anxiety, Panic, and Stress and Reclaim Joy

Boost Your Self-Esteem and Confidence

No! Why 'No' is the New 'Yes'

More of Cassandra's practical and inspiring books on a range of life enhancing topics can be found on her website (www. cassandragaisford.com) and her author page at all good online bookstores.

ABOUT THE TRANSFORMATIONAL SUPER KIDS SERIES

From the bestselling author of *The Little Princess* comes a brilliant new series, *Transformational Super Kid*s.

These young heroes and heroines tackle modern-day problems with the passion and gusto of warriors.

They defeat cruel critics, they slay savage self-esteem demons, and they show people—jealous of their kindness, talent, and beauty—that their biggest superpower is staying true to themselves.

Suitable for 'kids' of all ages. After all, aren't we all still children at heart?

PRAISE FOR THE TRANSFORMATIONAL SUPERKIDS

"Delightful and uplifting. . .

Lulu is a black sheep is a delightful and empowering story for our times! Uplifting messages woven throughout. A feel good story most will relate to, especially grown ups! Another one to add to your collection of Cassandra's self empowerment books! Thank you Cassandra!Delightful and uplifting!"

~ Heather Dodge

"Being released from the trauma. . .

This story is about the gaining of true power in growing into one's true self through childhood pain, discovering a new way of being, and knowing how where to go to gain help with being released from the trauma that had become one boys life. It is in the Author's Notes that this story transforms from a book to help children into a valuable resource for therapist and others who work with boys of all ages. Cassandra has captured a very typical aspect of how many boys are parented and the resulting chaos that becomes their adult-self. For those of us fortunate enough to have the privilege of working with men (boys of all ages) this sad yet beautiful story is one to keep handy and to share broadly.

~ Catherine Sloan, Counsellor and Intuitive Therapist

"Such a powerful message...

Sadly beautiful and a real reflection of our current society, which if we are really honest has lost direction, particularly with regards family values. Training in family values is an absolute pre-requisite before change will occur. I took pleasure in finding out the boy who cried not only survived but was blessed following the day the tears stopped and he found contentment, grace, and peace. My prayer is we can only attempt to save many more such boys."

~ Kenn Butler, CEO

"A wonderful tool...
This book is a wonderful tool for anyone seeking to begin the journey to self-reflection and healing from difficult childhoods. Therapists will find this book useful for their patients young or old. To return as a child to discover where the source of the pain begins has always been valuable, but actually relating it to present day is key to understanding. Highly recommended."

~ Alma Hammond, Author

"Helping children overcome negativity..

Billy is a Balloon is a lovely short story that is easy for children to read and very uplifting. The imagery of the lightness of a balloon rising above teasing, unkind words and self doubt is very powerful.

~ Laura Virgo

EXCERPT: THE LITTLE PRINCESS

PRAISE FOR THE LITTLE PRINCESS

"A Little Book with a Powerful Message...
An important reminder to always be true to yourself and summon the courage to follow your passions... Only *you* can live your life...GO live it!"

~ Harley

"The Little Princess is my hero…
I am a Midlife Coach, which means I help women find their moxie to do what they might not have done in the first half of their lives...I think *The Little Princess* needs to be a "required reading" text book for us all...she cuts to the heart of the lesson all of us need to hear, over and over again. *The Little Princess* embodies courage. She is my hero."

~ Sheree Clarke, Midlife Courage Coach

***"The Little Princess* is 'brilliant…**
Short concise & full of tremendous vision & wisdom, expressed lovingly. Many of the comments read truc for my

own journey. I recognize my passion to be different than many others, my persistence to succeed, & the pure joy I have at the end of each day when I lay down my head & give thanks."

~ Kenn Butler, CEO

"Very uplifting and inspiring…
I love everything Cassandra writes, the queen of uplifting inspiration! This is a little book, the story basically teaches you to have faith in your dreams, stand firm and don't let others rain on your parade.. We are all searching for purpose and passion, everybody hurts and sometimes we find ourselves on the receiving end of somebody else's insecurities, when they project their anger, jealousy etc onto us.. The old woman who puts the little princess down is really just jealous and stuck in her own life."

~ Reviewer UK

"A reminder of the truth in all of us…
The Little Princess is a great short story as a reminder of the truth in all of us; Don't judge, take loving kindness as a guideline in life, but stay true to yourself; A powerful message! Like all the books by this author, it is a guideline to live a wise life."

~ Maartje Jager, Designer

1

—————

Once upon a time there was a young woman who wanted to make a difference in the world.

She wanted to help others. She wanted to help people overcome depression, anxiety, and feeling sad.

She wanted to to help them feel inspired, joyful and happy.

She just wasn't sure how.

2

One day she had an inspired idea. "I can help people find their passion and purpose," she thought.

Her heart fluttered then soared higher and higher and higher—far, far, far away.

Almost beyond the reach of her doubts and fears.

She felt so excited—but also scared. She decided to feel the fear and create something anyway.

She knew people often struggled to find the time to read, and she wanted to make it easy and fun for people to find inspiration and help.

She decided to design a pack of inspirational cards that would enable people to help themselves and become empowered to transform their lives.

The cards would give people ideas, encourage them to dream, and give them hope.

She thought about the angel cards that had given her so much relief when she was an anxious child.

"Wouldn't it be fun to create something similar?" she thought.

Each card would have an inspirational quote on one side and a self-help strategy on the other.

DID YOU ENJOY THIS EXCERPT?

Grab your own copy of *The Little Princess*.
Follow your heart! Heed the call for courage.

Feeling stuck, depressed or demotivated? There are so many reasons why you should follow your dreams. If you need some motivation, look no further than this book.

Part moral allegory and part spiritual autobiography, *The Little Princess* is a timeless charm which tells the story of a young woman who leaves the safety of fitting in with everyone else, to follow her heart.

Be inspired by this journey to transformation and self-acceptance, and self-belief as she learns to overcome the vagaries of adult behaviour. Her personal odyssey culminates in a voyage of self-belief, passion, and purpose.

From the best-selling author of Mid-Life Career Rescue, Stress Less and How to Find Your Passion and Purpose: a powerful, inspiring, and practical book about boosting resilience, overcoming obstacles and moving forward after life's inevitable setbacks.

Find out what strategies are sabotaging your success. Find and follow your passion and purpose faster.

The Little Princess is available in audio, eBook, Hardcover and Paperback from all great online retailers.

COPYRIGHT

Copyright © 2020 Cassandra Gaisford
Published by Blue Giraffe Publishing 2020

Blue Giraffe Publishing is a division of Worklife Solutions Ltd.

Cover Design and Illustration by Cassandra Gaisford

rendering professional advice or services to the individual reader. The ideas, procedures, and suggestions contained in this book are not intended as a substitute for psychotherapy, counselling, or consulting with your physician.

The intent of the author is only to offer information of a general nature to help you in your quest for emotional, physical, and spiritual well-being.

Any use of information in this book is at the reader's discretion and risk. Neither the author nor the publisher can be held responsible for any loss, claim or damage arising out of the use, or misuse, of the suggestions made, the failure to take medical advice or for any material on third party websites.

First published by Blue Giraffe Publishing 2020

ISBN PRINT: 978-1-99-002034-6
ISBN EBOOK: 978-1-99-002033-9
ISBN HARDBACK: 978-1-99-002035-3